To my wonderful sisters,
Angela and Tessa

Henry Holt and Company, *Publishers since 1866*
Henry Holt® is a registered trademark of Macmillan Publishing Group, LLC
120 Broadway, New York, NY 10271 · mackids.com

Copyright © 2020 by Frann Preston-Gannon
All rights reserved.
Library of Congress Cataloging-in-Publication Data is available.
ISBN 978-1-250-13339-7
Our books may be purchased in bulk for promotional, educational, or business use. Please contact your local bookseller or the Macmillan Corporate
and Premium Sales Department at (800) 221-7945 ext. 5442 or by email at MacmillanSpecialMarkets@macmillan.com.
First edition, 2020
Design by Mallory Grigg
The illustrations were rendered using a mixture of acrylics, inks, and pencils, and then collaged and layered digitally.
Printed in China by Hung Hing Off-set Printing Co. Ltd., Heshan City, Guangdong Province
10 9 8 7 6 5 4 3 2 1

DANDYLION SUMMER

Frann Preston-Gannon

Henry Holt and Company
New York

On the last day of school,
my sister and I find a dandelion on the walk home.

We send the seeds off into the breeze

to find places to grow,

and we wish for the best summer ever.

Our wish carries on the wind,

through the town, into the park.

It swirls above the fields

filled with more flowers

than we have ever seen.

Then our wish comes true

in the most unexpected way.

Suddenly, a lion sits before us,

as lovely as the first breath of summer.

We decide to call him Dandylion.

We want to stay with him in the park,

but Mama is calling us home.

We follow Mama back to our house.

Little does she know, we are not alone.

When we get to our room,

Dandylion waits, curious,

just outside our window . . .

. . . until we decide

to let him in.

Each day,

Dandylion joins us in the garden.

And at night, he rests
beneath our window
under the summer moon.

My sister says a wish like this isn't

for keeping to yourself—

it's best shared with friends.

I am so happy. I want to play with Dandylion forever.

But some things

start to change.

The leaves turn red and gold and brown,

and the days grow colder.

Dandylion falls behind.

We see him less and less.

Until one day, he's gone, taking summer with him.

I feel sad, but my sister tells me not to worry.

She says Dandylion will be back one day.

So will summer.

And we have so many

new things to discover.

Together.